MIDNIGHT NINJA

SAM LLOYD

BLOOMSBURY
CHILDREN'S BOOKS
LONDON · OXFORD · NEW YORK · NEW DELHI · SYDNEY

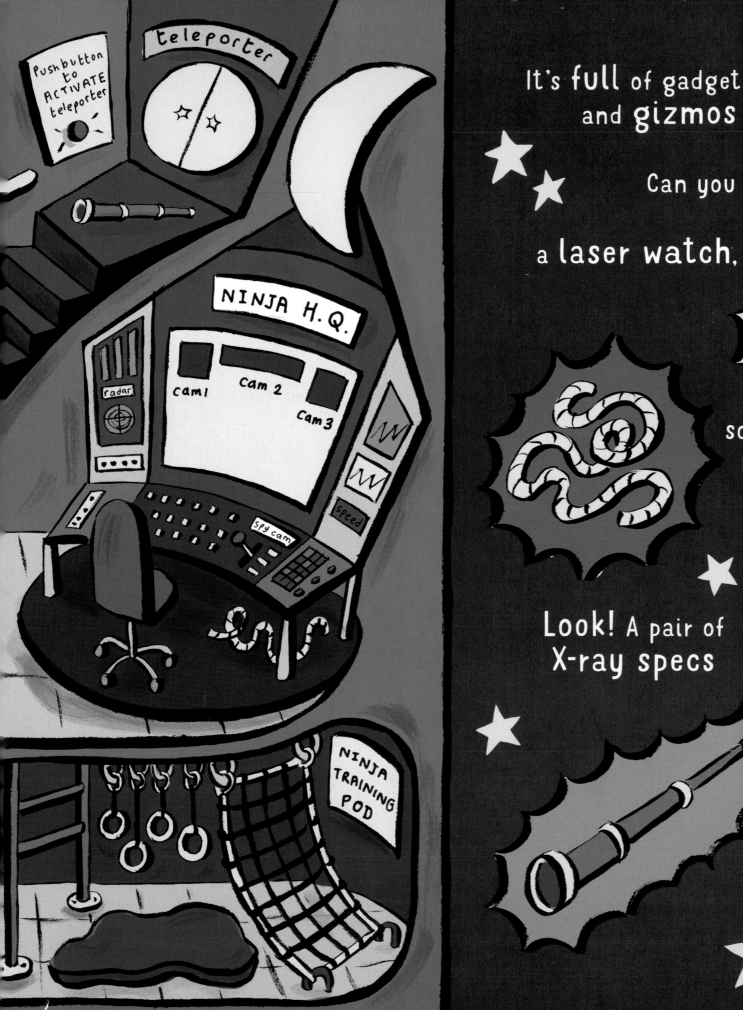

It's **full** of gadgets, techy things and **gizmos** all about.

Can you spot

a **laser watch**,
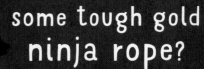

some tough gold **ninja rope?**

Look! A pair of **X-ray specs**
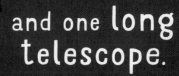

and one **long telescope.**

Uh-oh! Right through the telescope,
a very **frightening thing** ...

Look!
Sock-wearing spiders
and a BIG BAD
SPIDER KING.

His NINJA MISSION:

SAVE THE SOCKS!

"Watch me!
It won't take long.
I'm such a **cool**,
ace **ninja**
that nothing
will go wrong."

Ninja throws his hook up high – he climbs the temple wall.

Ninja **TIPTOES.**

Ninja
SPINS,

then

CRASH!

OH NO,

A FALL!

ZAPS!

Poor Midnight Ninja
with his **sticky** spider trap.

Back home,
old Ginger's worried,
Midnight Ninja's been
too long. He's got
a funny feeling
that **something**
must be wrong.

Eek! The spy cam
shows him that
his best friend
is in **need.**
And Ginger has
the answer . . .

NINJA H.Q.

Ketchup

How to cook a Ninja

SPY CAM

SECRET NINJA

So Ginger moves his neck-scarf,
and does a ninja bow. Then –

BISH

Their socks fly off!
He's cool, old Ginger. Wow!

Then Ginger looks from side to side
and from his dainty paws,
he shoots a special weapon . . .

HIYAH!

He slices through
the net
to set his best
friend **free**.

"I saved the socks!"
shouts Ninja.
"Just look at
clever me!"

"We're sorry,"
says the Spider King.
(He knows that stealing's silly.)

"Can you help us, Midnight Ninja?
Little spider feet get chilly."

The spiders love their silky socks,
"Midnight Ninja, you're SO great!"

So watch them zoom, and watch them fly –
"To Goody World – let's go!"
Returning all the stolen socks . . .

GO, MIDNIGHT NINJA, GO!

So, now you've met this little boy
and his pussycat called Ginger.

And you know his bedtime secret –
he's the mighty Midnight Ninja.

But can you keep the secret?
Don't let anybody know!
When those naughty baddies strike, it's . . .

GO, MIDNIGHT NINJA, GO!